little Miss Sunshine

by Roger Hargreaves

PSS!
PRICE STERN SLOAN
An Imprint of Penguin Group (USA) Inc.

Welcome to Miseryland.

We say "Welcome" but there really isn't very much welcoming about it.

It's the most miserable place in the world.

Miseryland worms look like this!

And when the birds wake up in the morning in Miseryland, they don't start singing.

They start crying!

Oh, it really is an awful place!

And the king of Miseryland is even worse.

He sits on his throne all day long with tears streaming down his face.

"Oh, I'm so unhappy," he keeps sobbing, over and over and over again.

Dear, oh dear, oh dear!

Little Miss Sunshine had been on vacation.

She'd had a lovely time, and now she was
driving home.

She was whistling happily to herself as she drove
along when, out of the corner of her eye,
she saw a sign.

TO MISERYLAND.

"Miseryland?" she asked herself.
"I've never heard of that before!"

And she headed down the road leading
to Miseryland.

She came to a sign that read:

YOU ARE NOW ENTERING MISERYLAND
      SMILING
      LAUGHING
      CHUCKLING
      GIGGLING
      FORBIDDEN
      By Order of the King.

Oh dear, thought Little Miss Sunshine as she drove along.

She came to a castle with a huge door.

A soldier stopped her.

"What do you want?" he asked gloomily.

"I want to see the king," smiled Little Miss Sunshine.

"You're under arrest," said the soldier.

"But why?" asked Little Miss Sunshine.

"For a very serious crime," replied the soldier. "Very serious indeed!"

The soldier marched Little Miss Sunshine through the huge door.

And across a courtyard.

And through another huge door.

And up an enormous staircase.

And along a long corridor.

And through another huge door.

And into a gigantic room.

And at the end of the gigantic room sat the king.

Crying his eyes out!

"Your Majesty," said the soldier, bowing low, "I have arrested this person for a very serious crime!"

The king stopped crying.

"She smiled at me," said the soldier.

There was a shocked silence.

"She did WHAT?" cried the king.

"She smiled at me," repeated the soldier.

"But why is smiling not allowed?"
laughed Little Miss Sunshine.

"She LAUGHED at me," cried the king.

"Why not?" she chuckled.

"She CHUCKLED!" wailed the king.

Little Miss Sunshine giggled.

"She GIGGLED!" blubbered the king.

And he burst into tears again.

"But why are these things not allowed?"
asked Little Miss Sunshine.

"Because this is Miseryland," wept the king.
"And they've never been allowed," he sobbed.
"Oh, I was so unhappy before you arrived," he
wailed, "but now I'm twice as unhappy!"

Little Miss Sunshine looked at him.

"But wouldn't you like to be happy?" she asked.

"Of course I would," cried the king.
"But how can I be? This is MISERYLAND!"

Little Miss Sunshine thought.

"Come on," she said.

"You can't talk to me like that," sobbed the king.

"Don't be silly," she replied, and led him across the gigantic room, and through the huge door, and along the long corridor, and down the enormous staircase, and through the huge door, and across the courtyard, and through the huge door to her car.

"Get in," she said.

Little Miss Sunshine drove the crying king back to the large Miseryland sign.

"Dry your eyes," she said, and handed him a large handkerchief from her purse.

And then, from her purse, she pulled out a large pen.

Five minutes later she'd finished.

Instead of the sign reading:

YOU ARE NOW ENTERING MISERYLAND
    SMILING
    LAUGHING
    CHUCKLING
    GIGGLING
    FORBIDDEN
    By Order of the King.

Do you know what it read?

YOU ARE NOW ENTERING LAUGHTERLAND
      SMILING
      LAUGHING
      CHUCKLING
      GIGGLING
      PERMITTED
      By Order of the King.

"There," said Little Miss Sunshine. "Now you can be happy."

"But I don't know HOW to be happy," sniffed the king. "I've never TRIED it!"

"Nonsense," said Little Miss Sunshine. "It's really very easy," she smiled.

The king tried a smile.

"Not bad," she laughed.

The king tried a laugh.

"Getting better," she chuckled.

The king tried a chuckle.

"You've got it," she giggled.

The king looked at her.

"So I have," he giggled. "I'm the king of Laughterland!"

As Little Miss Sunshine arrived home, there was Mr. Happy out for an evening stroll.

"Hello," he grinned. "Where have you been?"

"Miseryland!" she replied.

"Miseryland?" he said. "I didn't know there was such a place!"

Little Miss Sunshine giggled.

"Actually," she said.

"There isn't!"